A Note from Michelle about the Ghost in My Closet

Hi! I'm Michelle Tanner. I'm nine years old. And I have never been more scared in my entire life! It all started when I went to see this spooky film, *Haunted Houseful*. Ever since then, some really strange things have been going on around the house. Now I'm sure there's a ghost in my closet! But there's no such thing as a ghost—is there? No one in my family thinks so. And I have a *big* family!

There's my dad and my two older sisters, D.J. and Stephanie. But that's not all.

My mom died when I was little. So my uncle Jesse moved in to help take care of us. So did Joey Gladstone. He's my dad's friend from college. It's almost like having three dads. But that's still not all!

First Uncle Jesse got married to Becky Donaldson. Then they had twin boys, Nicky and Alex. The twins are four years old now. And they're so cute.

That's nine people. Our dog, Comet, makes ten. (The ghost makes eleven!) Sure, it gets kind of crazy sometimes. But I wouldn't change it for anything. It's so much fun to live in a full house—minus one ghost!

FULL HOUSE™ MICHELLE novels

The Great Pet Project
The Super-Duper Sleepover Party
My Two Best Friends
Lucky, Lucky Day
The Ghost in My Closet

Available from MINSTREL Books

FULL HOUSE™
Michelle

The Ghost in My Closet

Cathy East Dubowski

A Parachute Press Book

A MINSTREL® BOOK

Published by POCKET BOOKS
New York   London   Toronto   Sydney   Tokyo   Singapore

A MINSTREL PAPERBACK *Original*

A Minstrel Book published by
POCKET BOOKS, a division of Simon & Schuster Inc.
1230 Avenue of the Americas, New York, NY 10020

A PARACHUTE PRESS BOOK

READING Copyright © 1995 by Warner Bros. Television

FULL HOUSE, characters, names and all related indicia are trademarks of Warner Bros. Television © 1995.

ISBN: 0-671-53573-0

First Minstrel Books printing November 1995

10 9 8 7 6 5 4 3 2 1

A MINSTREL BOOK and colophon are registered trademarks of Simon & Schuster Inc.

Cover photo copyright © 1994 Dualstar Entertainment Group, Inc.

Printed in the U.S.A.

The Ghost in My Closet

Chapter

1

♥ Nine-year-old Michelle Tanner's hand froze in her buttered popcorn. She stared up at the movie screen with big, round eyes.

A girl with curly red hair played with her dolls on her pretty pink bed. But something awful was going to happen. Michelle just knew it! She could tell by the music: *BOOM boom BOOM boom BOOM boom BOOM* . . .

Michelle covered her face with her hands. The music swelled. Got faster. Louder. Drums pounded. Violins shrieked: *Scree! Scree! Scree! Scree!*

Michelle couldn't help it. She *had* to see what was happening now! Nervously she peeked through her fingers.

The camera zoomed in on the space beneath the girl's bed. The ruffle rustled. Two eyes glowed in the dusty dark.

Then a slimy green claw slid out from under the bed!

Michelle sank down in her squeaking seat and hugged her popcorn box like a teddy bear.

Now the claw was crawling up the side of the spread. Slowly . . . toward the girl's ankle.

Look out! Michelle wanted to shout. *Run!* Instead she squeezed her eyes shut and ducked. She covered her ears when the girl screamed—in earsplitting stereo!

Suddenly—an icy claw grabbed Michelle in the dark!

"Aaaagghh!" Michelle screamed. "It's got me!" She jerked away. Popcorn flew everywhere.

"Sorry, Michelle!"

Michelle brushed her bangs out of her eyes and stared. The icy hand belonged to her sister. "Stephanie! Don't do that. You scared me half to death!"

A bony finger poked her in the back. Michelle jumped.

"Shhhhh!" whispered a woman sitting behind them.

"Sorry," Michelle mumbled.

Michelle brushed the popcorn off her pink-and-blue sweatshirt. She shivered. But she didn't have the chills just because the theater was cold.

She had the chills because *Haunted Houseful* was the scariest movie she'd ever seen. *Even Stephanie looks scared,* Michelle thought. *And she's thirteen!*

On the other side of her sat Joey Gladstone. He was a comedian on a morning radio show and her dad's best friend. He had moved in to help out when Michelle's mother died. That was when she was a baby. It was almost like having another father. Except Joey often acted as goofy as the boys in fourth grade!

Like now. Joey covered his face with one hand. He pulled his knees up to his chin. The ice in his soda cup rattled noisily. He pretended to shake with fright!

"Michelle!" he whispered loudly. "Tell me when the scary part's over."

"The whole movie's the scary part," Michelle whispered back.

She knew Joey was just trying to be funny—trying to make her feel better. But even he couldn't make her laugh now.

Michelle curled up in her seat. She stopped looking at the screen. She played dot-to-dot on her pink polka-dot leggings instead. But she could still hear every word.

"Daddy! Help me!" the girl in the movie screamed.

"Bill!" her terrified mother cried. *"Do something!"*

But even Joey settled down as the music grew soft and haunting. Up on-screen the redheaded girl woke up. It was almost midnight. She heard noises in the kitchen. Slowly she crept downstairs.

A single candle flickered on the table. Her father was stirring a bubbling pot on the stove. Then he dipped out a cupful of the smoking brew and handed it to her older sister.

Scree! Scree! Scree! Scree!

The figure turned. It *wasn't* her sister. It was a ghost with a glowing, skull-like face and moldy, snakelike hair!

Sobbing, the redheaded girl flung herself into her father's arms. But his arms weren't warm and loving tonight. They were as cold as ice and clutched at her, tighter and tighter. The girl looked up—and screamed. The candlelight flickered across his face.

Scree! Scree! Scree! Scree! The haunted house had turned her father into a zombie!

Michelle pulled her sweatshirt up over her face. Only her strawberry blond ponytail stuck out. "Don't look," she told herself. "It's almost over, it's almost over . . ."

Haunted Houseful seemed to go on for hours. But at last it *was* over.

The credits rolled, and the lights came back on. All around her sat regular people. No monsters or ghosts or witches. They joked and chatted as they stood up to leave.

Still, Michelle clung to Joey's hand as they hurried up the aisle and out to the street.

"Wow," said Joey. "That movie gave my goose bumps goose bumps!" He put his fists to his chest. He flapped his elbows up and down. "Braaack! Braaack! Just call me Chicken Joe from now on!"

He looked so silly strutting up and down the sidewalk. Michelle and Stephanie giggled. So did some people walking by.

Laughing made Michelle feel better. She

didn't feel so scared anymore. But on the way to the car, she still held on tight to Joey's hand.

A chilly October breeze swirled dry, dead leaves around their feet. Clouds darkened the sky.

Michelle's eyes strayed to the shops they passed. A skeleton wind sock dangled by a door, waving its bony arms and legs. In another window, toothless monsters and gory ghouls stared blindly at her—rubber Halloween masks for sale.

Michelle was glad when they finally reached the car. She made Stephanie sit in the backseat with her.

Joey laughed. "Hey, I feel like your chauffeur!"

But Michelle's spooky mood was no joke. *How long will it last?* Michelle wondered. *How long till the scary feelings go away?*

Chapter
2

♥ That night the Tanner household gathered around the dinner table. There was Michelle's father, Danny, of course. And Joey, too. Plus her sisters, Stephanie and D.J.

Across the table sat her uncle Jesse. He was a rock singer and co-host of Joey's radio show. He and his wife, Becky, lived in the attic. They had twin four-year-old boys named Nicky and Alex.

That made nine people living in one house.

"Woof!" the Tanners' dog, Comet,

begged for food. He picked the best spot, too: next to the twins' chairs. Comet wasn't exactly a "people." But he made ten.

Michelle grinned. How could she possibly be scared in such a full house?

Danny Tanner plunked down a covered casserole in the middle of the table. He jerked off the lid and waved his flowered oven mitt in the air. "Ta-da!"

Steam rose from the dish. Everyone stared, bug-eyed.

Michelle's dad loved to experiment with new recipes. Sometimes things turned out great! Other times they turned out . . . weird. Like now.

Joey peered at the casserole. "Eeeeewwww! This looks like something from the movie we saw today!" He dug out a couple of drippy spoonfuls. "Yu-u-u-m!"

Michelle gulped. Why did he have to remind her?

Joey turned to Michelle. "Monster stew," he said in a haunted-house voice. "Try it. You vill like it!"

Everyone at the table laughed. Even the twins. But not Michelle.

"No, thanks!" she said. She had just lost her appetite.

In fact, just thinking about that awful movie made her feel sick to her stomach!

After supper Michelle went into the living room to watch TV with the rest of the family. Everyone voted to tune in to the nature special.

Michelle watched the first few minutes. Then she decided she didn't want to see the rest. It was all about bats. And bats made her think about haunted houses!

So Michelle went upstairs to read.

Creeeek! The third step from the bottom groaned when she stepped on it. She'd have to remember to skip it.

Upstairs she flicked on the hall light. She stared at the old black-and-white photograph of Great-great-grandmother Tanner hanging on the wall. She'd never noticed before how weird it was. The eyes seemed to follow you wherever you went. Just like the paintings in the movie.

Michelle stopped looking and hurried down the hall. She and Stephanie shared a bedroom. Usually it was a pretty rowdy place. But the room was dark and silent now. Stephanie was still downstairs watching bat TV.

Michelle flipped the wall switch. It turned on the pretty lamp that sat on the table next to her bed. Beside the lamp was the book she'd been reading, *Ghost Stories from Around the World.*

Michelle curled up on her bed. She wondered if she should pick another book tonight. She flipped it open. Only two chapters left. *I might as well finish,* she thought.

Before long she forgot about everything except the stories in her book. They were exciting. She couldn't put them down. They really weren't so scary after all.

Suddenly the lights began to flicker on and off. Then Michelle's room plunged into darkness.

A light clicked on in the middle of the room. A flashlight.

Michelle shrieked as the flashlight shone on a face. A glowing, skull-like face with stringy hair. A second later she breathed a sigh of relief. Stephanie had the flashlight pressed up under her chin. Eerie shadows made Stephanie look like that horrible creature in the movie.

"Welcome to *Haunted Houseful,*" Stephanie said. Her voice sounded deep and sinister. "The house of your dreams— or should I say nightmares!"

"Stephanie!" Michelle grumbled. "Cut it out."

Stephanie just laughed. The flashlight bobbed across the dark room. "Hey, Michelle, look at my hand." She held her hand in front of the beam. Red light seemed to burn right through her sister's fingers. Michelle thought she could almost see Stephanie's bones!

"Stephanie . . . turn on the lights. Please?"

"Okay, okay." Stephanie flipped on the light. "Don't be such a scaredy-cat."

"I'm not a scaredy-cat!" Michelle shot back.

Stephanie shrugged. "Dad said to tell you half-hour warning till bedtime. Better go brush your teeth."

Glad to, Michelle said to herself. *If I can just get them to stop chattering!*

Michelle got ready for bed . . . very slowly. Maybe she'd get lucky. Maybe the sun would come up before they had to turn out the light!

Michelle climbed into bed. She wondered if Stephanie was thinking about the movie too. She peeked over at her sister.

Nope. Stephanie was dancing to the

radio as she picked out clothes for school the next day. She didn't look worried or scared at all.

I'd better not say anything, Michelle decided. *Stephanie might make fun of me for being scared.*

Danny came in to kiss them both good night. "Michelle, you're still up?" he asked.

"Yeah," Michelle replied, "but I'm starting to get sleepy."

"Okay," her dad said. "Boy, I'm bushed. I think I'll go on to bed and read a little. You girls need me for anything?"

Yes! Michelle wanted to shout. *To keep the ghosts away!*

"No, we're fine," Stephanie chirped happily. She gave him a quick kiss. "Good night, Dad!"

Danny left. Stephanie clicked off the light.

"Good night, Michelle," Stephanie said with a big yawn.

"Night . . ." Michelle said softly. She pulled up the covers. She waited for her eyes to get used to the dark. Her teddy bear night-light barely shone. Maybe it needed a new bulb.

Michelle never had trouble falling asleep—most of the time. But tonight was different. Tonight she couldn't stop thinking about that movie! She knew the story was made up. The monsters and ghosts were just actors—or big special-effects puppets. None of the blood or slime was real. The whole movie was as fake as a Halloween costume.

But sometimes costumes could seem awfully real.

Drip! . . . Drip! . . . Drip!

Water dripped in the bathroom sink across the hall. But Michelle felt too chicken to get up and turn it off.

Ticktock, ticktock, ticktock . . .

The grandfather clock in the hallway ticked away the minutes.

Drip-tock! Drip-tock!

Creaaaak!

A floorboard creaked somewhere. As if somebody—or something—was creeping around the house.

Michelle wrapped the covers up around her ears. She felt like a mummy. *Don't think about mummies!* she told herself. But at least she couldn't hear the spooky sounds anymore.

At last she drifted off to sleep.

Thump!

Michelle sat up in bed. What was that?

She peered over at Stephanie's bed. But Stephanie was fast asleep. One leg stuck out from the covers. It dangled over the edge of the bed.

Click! A picture popped into Michelle's mind, as sharp and clear as a slide show. A picture of the green claw grabbing the redheaded girl's ankle.

She shook her head to clear it.

Then she tried not to move. She tried not to breathe. She listened hard.

The house was totally silent. What time was it, anyway?

Michelle sighed and lay back down. "Just go to sleep!" she scolded herself. "This is a normal house. And those are normal sounds."

She took a deep breath and pulled the covers up to her chin. She made herself think about nice things. Like birthday parties . . . Rollerblades . . . pizza with all the toppings—

SLAM!

The front door!

Michelle froze in her bed.

Footsteps.

She heard footsteps!

For real!

Michelle ducked under the covers.

Someone was creeping up the stairs!

Chapter

3

♥ The footsteps crept closer. They stopped right outside Michelle's open bedroom door.

Michelle held her breath. She peeked out from under the covers with one eye.

Was that a head . . . fl-floating in her darkened doorway?

She tried to scream. She opened her mouth. But nothing came out. (She was too scared!)

"Psst!" The voice came from the head in the doorway. "Stephanie—are you asleep?"

Michelle groaned. "D.J.!"

Now she remembered. D.J. went to study over at a friend's house tonight. She had a big history test tomorrow. D.J. was eighteen. So she was allowed to stay out late. Even on a school night.

D.J. tiptoed over. She sat on Michelle's bed. "Sorry, Michelle. Did I wake you up?"

"That's okay." Michelle put her hand on her chest. Her heart was beating hard. She felt as if she had just run the relay race at school.

"Listen," D.J. whispered. "In the morning tell Stephanie I want my purple sweater back. Okay? I want to wear it tomorrow. And it better be clean!"

She kissed Michelle on the top of the head. Then she tiptoed down the hall to her own room.

Michelle snuggled back down in her covers. She listened to Stephanie's quiet breathing. For once she was glad she had to share a room!

Maybe now she could fall asleep. . . .

Plop!

Something big and squishy landed on Michelle's head.

She shoved it off and sat up.

It was Stephanie's favorite pillow.

Michelle rubbed her eyes and looked around.

Hey! she thought. *It's morning!* Sunlight streamed in her bedroom window. Stephanie was already awake and dressed.

"Better get up, sleepyhead," Stephanie teased. She brushed out her long blond hair. "No telling what Dad's cooked up for breakfast!"

She stopped at the doorway and grinned. "Shall I tell him you're on your way down?"

Michelle just yawned and threw off her covers. When had she fallen asleep? She had no idea. But it must have been pretty late. She was still sleepy!

She pulled on some clothes. She ran a comb through her hair and brushed her teeth. Then she dashed downstairs to the kitchen.

Aunt Becky flashed her a quick smile. "Morning, Michelle." She was trying to feed Alex and Nicky some oatmeal. They were trying to finger-paint with it—on each other's faces.

Uncle Jesse was trying to take a picture of them. "Look, Michelle. Aren't they *sooo* cute?"

Michelle smiled and sat down between her sisters.

"Hi, honey," her dad called out. He was holding two plates. "Do you want the egg-foo-yung omelet or the brownie pancakes?"

"Psst! Take the pancakes!" D.J. hissed from behind her history book.

Stephanie nodded and sneaked her omelet to Comet.

Joey came upstairs just then. His room was downstairs. It used to be the basement, but he turned it into an apartment. It was nice, but he kept a lot of weird stuff lying around.

"Want to hear my new jokes?" Joey asked everybody. He was wearing silly plastic glasses with a fake nose and mustache.

Joey's disguise made Michelle think about the Halloween masks she saw the day before. And that made her think about monsters in the movie. But . . . hey! She didn't feel scared!

Michelle sighed happily. Nothing like a nice normal Tanner morning to chase the scaries away!

Why was I so afraid last night? she wondered. It seemed so silly now that it was daytime.

Maybe her teacher, Mrs. Yoshida, was

right about her. She always said Michelle had an "active imagination"!

Michelle made up her mind. No fake blood and creepy special effects were going to ruin her day. She was going to forget about that silly old movie—right then and there!

For a while that worked. Michelle *didn't* think about *Haunted Houseful* all day at school. She had a spelling test and missed only one word. Broccalee. (Broccoly? Broccoli!) She didn't like to *eat* broccoli. So she didn't mind too much that she couldn't *spell* it.

She and her best friend, Cassie Wilkins, ate lunch together. They used colored markers to make their other best friend, Mandy Metz, a get-well card. She was home with the flu.

That afternoon Mrs. Yoshida told the class they were going on a field trip next week.

All in all, it was a pretty cheery day.

After school Michelle stopped by Mandy's house. Mandy didn't feel well, Mrs. Metz said. And she didn't want Michelle to catch the flu. So Michelle just gave Mrs. Metz the card and some homework assignments for Mandy.

At home Michelle finished her homework early. She and Stephanie turned on the TV. Reruns of their favorite sitcom started at four-thirty. In three minutes they were laughing out loud.

Then a commercial came on. Michelle's laughter died.

"Hey," said Stephanie. "Look! It's that movie we went to see yesterday."

The commercial showed some of the scariest parts.

If only I had seen the commercial before! Michelle thought. *I never would have gone to see that stupid movie!*

"Uh . . . how about a snack?" Michelle said. She backed out of the room. Comet followed, wagging his tail.

Michelle searched the fridge and the kitchen cabinets. She wanted something good. Something that didn't look like anything in that movie!

At last she decided on two chocolate chip muffins. She got two plates. She put a muffin on each plate.

"Michelle!" Stephanie screamed. "Come here! Quick!"

Michelle ran into the living room. "What? What!"

"Oh, you missed it," said Stephanie. The sitcom was back on. "They showed that funny scene from *Haunted Houseful*. You know, the one where the family's Thanksgiving turkey starts jogging up and down the table. Remember?"

Yuck! thought Michelle. She was glad she hadn't seen that! She hurried back into the kitchen. Comet dashed out. "Tell her to change the channel," she muttered to the dog.

Michelle reached for the snacks she'd made.

But they were gone!

As if they'd walked right off the plate!

Michelle ran back into the living room. "Stephanie—!"

BAM!

The front door banged open. Leaves swirled across the living-room floor.

Michelle stared at the doorway.

No one was there.

Had the door opened all by itself?

Chapter 4

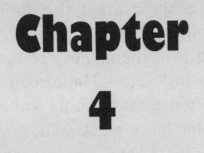 "AHHHHHHHHHHHH!" Michelle screamed.

Stephanie jumped up from the couch. "What in the world?"

"Hey!" Uncle Jesse straightened up in the doorway. He had just picked up a huge stack of boxes and bags. "Can somebody help me with these packages? I think there's a storm brewing!"

Michelle let out a huge sigh. *Doors don't open by themselves,* she reminded herself. *Not in real life.* She went over to help Uncle Jesse with the packages.

"Look at these great decorations I got for Halloween," Jesse said. "Alex and Nicky will love them. They're too little to remember last year's Halloween."

He started yanking things out of the boxes. A big hairy black spider on an elastic string. Black and orange crepe paper streamers. A ceramic skull with a black candle inside. And a witch costume complete with broom.

Jesse held a warty mask up to his face. "How do I look?"

Stephanie laughed. "Cool, Uncle Jesse!"

But Michelle shivered. He looked creepy to her!

"Heh, heh, heh!" Jesse cackled in a witchy voice. "I can't wait! I'm going to scare the pants off those little guys. They're gonna love it!"

A few minutes later Michelle ran to her room. She jumped onto her bed and hugged her stuffed panda. Her face was still red with embarrassment. *Stephanie* and Uncle Jesse must think I'm a total idiot!

A comic book! Michelle thought. *That's what I need to get my mind off scary things. A good laugh.* She rolled onto her stomach and leaned over the side of the mattress. That's where she stashed her old comics. Under the bed . . . where it was dark . . . and spidery . . . and creepy. The kind of place where slimy green claws reached out and grabbed you.

"On second thought—never mind."

She hopped off the bed to search for somebody—anybody—she could hang out with. Maybe the twins would play with her. It didn't matter. As long as she didn't have to be alone.

At dinner Michelle slipped most of her food to Comet. He didn't seem to mind that the olives looked like little green eyeballs. He even ate the red stuff in the middle!

Scratch. Scratch. Scratch.

Michelle's eyes jerked toward the window.

Halloween was over a week away. But Uncle Jesse had already taped a cardboard black cat to the windowpane.

Scratch. Scratch. Scratch.

Was someone out there in the dark?

Scratch. Scratch. Scratch.

Or was it just those branches blowing against the glass?

She glanced around the table. No one else seemed to notice. They were all too busy listening to Jesse. He was telling them about the new Halloween song he had written for the kids. Alex and Nicky were trying to hum it.

"What's the matter, Michelle?" D.J. asked. "You look like you've just seen a ghost."

Michelle swallowed. Her sister D.J. was smart and nice—most of the time. Maybe she could talk to her about the spooky things going on in the house. "D.J.—" Michelle began.

"Yes, Michelle?" D.J. speared the last olive and popped it into her mouth.

"Well," Michelle began. "I think maybe our house is—"

"Excuse me, honey." Danny reached across her to gather some dirty dishes. "Whose night is it to help clean up the kitchen?"

D.J. tried to make excuses.

Stephanie tried to sneak out.

"I'll help!" Michelle said quickly.

The whole room fell dead silent.

"Excuse me?" said D.J. "Michelle—you never volunteer in the kitchen."

"Well, I am now!" Michelle said. "And don't you dare try to stop me!"

"Okay, okay," her dad said. "Can't argue with that!"

Michelle was developing a bad case of the shivers. There was no way she was leaving her dad's side tonight!

*   *   *

Later that evening the doorbell rang. Danny went to answer it.

Michelle jumped up and followed him.

Danny stopped with his hand on the doorknob.

Michelle bumped into the back of his legs.

"Michelle," Danny joked, "I've always hoped we'd be close. But this is a little much."

Michelle smiled weakly and stepped back an inch.

Danny opened the door. An old woman stood in the shadows. Rain dripped from her crooked black umbrella.

"Hello?" Danny said.

The woman took a step forward into the light.

It was Miss Teasdale, from down the street. She was about a hundred years old, Michelle thought. In the darkness her old-fashioned black dress and shoes looked eerie.

"Good evening, Mr. Tanner," she said in a formal British accent. "I do hope I'm not disturbing you."

"Not at all, Miss Teasdale," said Danny. "Won't you come in?"

"Oh, no, no," she said, shaking her long, thin hand. A blood-red ruby ring sparkled in the porch light. The ring looked old, like something from a museum.

"Is there something we can do for you?" Danny asked.

"It's my cat," Miss Teasdale said. "She's gone—missing."

"Oh, that's terrible," said Danny. "What does she look like?"

Miss Teasdale smiled. "She's black. With a little white half-moon shape on her forehead. Green eyes. And smart as a whip! Her name is Midnight.

"Most folks are afraid of black cats," she added with a soft, dry laugh. "They think they're bad luck. But not I. In England we say it's the *white* cats that are

35

bad luck." She gazed down at Michelle. Her green eyes seemed full of secrets.

A shiver ran up Michelle's spine.

Then Miss Teasdale frowned. "It's very important that I find her," she said. "She's . . . well, let's just say she's having some problems that need my attention."

Danny turned to Michelle. "Have you seen the cat, Michelle?"

Michelle shook her head.

"We'll keep an eye out for her," Danny promised Miss Teasdale. "Let us know if she turns up."

"Thank you ever so much," Miss Teasdale said. "Good evening." With that she melted away into the rainy darkness.

That night Michelle tried to talk Stephanie into sleeping with the light on.

"Uh-uh," said Stephanie. "Sleeping with the light on can mess up your dreams."

"No way!" said Michelle.

"It's true! I read it in *Spunky* magazine." Stephanie snapped off the light.

"Wait!" cried Michelle. "I'm not ready!" She flipped the light back on. She dug in her drawer for her flashlight. She gathered all her stuffed animals, even the old ones from her bottom drawer. She closed the bedroom door all the way.

Then she closed her eyes and flipped off the light. Her feet barely touched the floor as she hurried across the room and into her bed.

I'm going to sleep sitting up, Michelle said to herself. She propped up her pillows. She tucked all her stuffed animals around her.

That is—if she could fall asleep at all!

"Stephanie?" Michelle whispered across the dark room.

No answer.

"Hey, Steph!"

"What?"

"Do you ever get scared?" Michelle asked.

"No!"

"Really?"

"Well," said Stephanie. "Sometimes, I guess."

"What do you do?" Michelle asked.

Stephanie yawned. "I just stop thinking about it. Now go to sleep."

Michelle sighed. She tried to stop thinking about the movie . . . with its ghosts, creepy claws, and zombie dads. She tried not to remember how the red-haired actress's screams seemed so real.

She tried to forget about her disappearing snack. The weird noises at dinner. The sounds in the middle of the night.

But that just made her think about them even more.

Plus, she kept seeing Miss Teasdale's eerie green eyes. Eyes the same color as those of her black cat, Midnight. . . .

And was that really true about black

cats in England? Or was Miss Teasdale just making it up?

Scratch! Scratch! Scratch!

Michelle's eyes flew open.

Something was making noises from inside the walls of her room! Scratching noises!

She definitely heard something. No kidding this time!

"Stephanie!" Michelle whispered. *"Steph! Wake up!"*

Stephanie jolted up in bed. "What? What's wrong?"

"Did you hear that?"

"What?"

"That noise!"

"What noise?"

"Stephanie!" Michelle cried. "That scratching noise!"

"No," said Stephanie. "I didn't hear a scratch. Please, Michelle. Go to sleep!"

Michelle tried. She tried till the clock in the hall chimed the hour.

Scratch. Scratch. Scratch.

"There it is again!" Michelle cried out loud.

"Wha—?" Stephanie sat up in her bed again. She was still half asleep.

"Woof! Woof! Rrrrrrrr!"

SCRATCH-SCRATCH-SCRATCH!

Stephanie jumped out of bed and flipped on the light. Then she flung open the bedroom door.

Comet ran in, barking wildly.

Stephanie rolled her eyes. "See, Michelle? It was only Comet. You shut our door and he was trying to come in."

Michelle frowned. "But that's not the same sound I heard before!"

Danny hurried into the room. "What's going on in here?"

A sleepy Uncle Jesse was right behind him. "Is everyone all right?" He had his robe half on and his slippers on the wrong feet. And he was carrying a small electric guitar like a club.

Comet barked and ran around in circles. He sniffed everything in sight.

"What's wrong with Comet?" Danny asked. "Come here, boy." Danny bent down on one knee and got the dog to come to him. Comet was crazy with excitement.

"You know, Comet has been acting a little odd lately," Danny pointed out. "He hasn't been eating his regular dog food at all."

"Joey said Comet threw up when he walked him this afternoon," Uncle Jesse added. "Maybe he's getting sick or something."

"I'd better take him to the vet tomorrow," Danny said. "I think I'll make him a bed in my bathroom. And shut him in. Just in case he feels sick again."

"Let me know if I can do anything," Jesse said. "Good night, girls." Yawning, he wandered out of the room.

"Is Comet going to be okay, Dad?" Stephanie asked.

"Don't worry," Danny said. "I'm sure he'll be fine." He gently led Comet out into the hall.

"Dad," Michelle piped up. "I need to talk to you."

Danny glanced at his watch. Comet kept straining against his dog collar, trying to get back into Michelle's room. "I'm sorry, Michelle. I've got to get Comet settled. Can it wait till the morning?"

"Sure, Dad," Michelle replied. She knew he was worried about Comet.

"You girls really need to get back to sleep," Danny added. "It's a school night, don't forget."

Stephanie rolled her eyes and giggled. "How could we forget that?"

Michelle and Stephanie settled back into bed again. Stephanie fell asleep almost immediately. But Michelle couldn't even close her eyes. She was more worried than ever.

Had Comet heard the same strange noises she had?

Was that why he was acting strange—because something strange was going on in the house?

Michelle tossed and turned for hours, thinking.

Scratch. Scratch. Scratch.

There was that sound again! And this time it couldn't be Comet. He was locked up in Danny's bedroom, at the other end of the hall.

Michelle lay in her bed, terrified. She was too scared to call out. She was too scared to go get her father.

Could it be . . . ?

Could the Tanner house really be haunted?

Chapter
5

♥ "Dad! I've got something to tell you!" Michelle said the next morning.

The Tanner kitchen was in an uproar. Breakfast was usually omelets or home-made coffee cake. Today it was Pop-Tarts in a paper towel.

Joey was shouting about being late for a meeting.

Aunt Becky was searching everywhere for a lost shoe.

Uncle Jesse was trying to undress the twins. He had put their shirts and pants on backward.

Stephanie was looking for her homework.

And D.J. was trying to put on some mascara, using the toaster for a mirror. When the toaster popped, she smeared makeup on her nose.

Michelle followed Danny back and forth across the kitchen. "Dad, please listen . . ."

"I am listening, honey," Danny said. "It's just that we're all late. None of our alarm clocks went off this morning."

"What do you mean?" said Michelle. "How come? Didn't you set them?"

Danny raced down the lineup of grown-ups. They held out their coffee cups, and Danny poured. "Of course we set them, honey. But the time is wrong on all the clocks. The electricity must have shut off sometime during the night. Maybe because of the storm."

"The electricity . . . !" Michelle gasped.

That proved it! Ghostly spirits were

playing in the walls. Driving Comet crazy. Turning off the electricity!

There was no doubt about it.

The Tanner house was haunted for sure!

"Dad! That's what I'm trying to tell you," Michelle said. "Our house is full of ghosts!"

"Great!" Danny said. He gave the kitchen counter one last wipe with the sponge. "Maybe they'll clean up the kitchen after we leave. Now we've all got to go or we'll be late for sure!"

Michelle gave up. *He doesn't believe me anyway,* she thought. *Nobody does.* She'd have to find a way to make somebody see.

Michelle sat at her desk in Mrs. Yoshida's fourth-grade classroom. She propped her elbow on her desk. Then she propped her head in her hand.

She was supposed to be reading. But her eyes wouldn't pay attention.

Slowly one eye slid shut. Michelle yawned. Slowly the other eye slid shut.

"Michelle!" Her friend Cassie gently pushed her shoulder. "Wake up!"

Michelle opened her eyes and shook her head.

"Why are you so tired today?" asked Cassie.

"Yeah," whispered her other friend, Lee. "Wake up, sleepyhead!"

Cassie giggled. But Michelle just frowned. Could she tell her friends the truth? Or would they just laugh at her?

"Ahem!" Mrs. Yoshida stared at them with one eyebrow raised. "This is supposed to be silent-reading time."

"Yes, ma'am," Michelle said. She propped up her book. Quickly she whispered to Cassie and Lee, "I'll tell you at lunch!"

Michelle sat at her favorite table in the cafeteria. The one with the view of the playground. She opened her lunch box. But she didn't feel like eating anything. She was too sleepy.

Soon Lee sat down with his paper lunch bag. "So—what's up?"

"We've got to wait till Cassie gets here," Michelle said.

Cassie's mom always made her eat a hot lunch from the cafeteria line.

"Oh, all right," Lee said. "Then show me what you've got for lunch. Want to trade desserts?"

At last Cassie sat down with her tray. "Okay, Michelle. Tell us. What's going on?"

Michelle took a deep breath. Then she blurted, "My house is haunted!"

"Oooohhh!" Cassie squealed.

"No way!" Lee said.

"I don't believe it," Cassie said.

"It's true!" Michelle insisted.

"Prove it," Lee said. "I dare you!"

"Fine!" Michelle said. She hoped she

sounded braver than she felt. She chewed a tiny bite of sandwich thoughtfully. "I've got an idea. But I'll have to ask my dad if it's okay."

Friday evening the Tanner doorbell rang. Danny opened the door.

Three people stood on the front porch. A pizza delivery boy with a ponytail was holding a huge pizza box. Cassie was wearing a black turtleneck and black sweatpants and holding a fishing net and a magnifying glass. Lee was dressed all in black too. He was also wearing his hockey goalie mask and holding a baseball bat.

"Did I miss something here?" Danny asked. "Halloween's not till *next* week—right?" He checked the date on his calendar watch, then shook his head. "I'm sorry, but we don't give out candy for dress rehearsals." He chuckled at his own joke. But no one else laughed.

Her father cleared his throat. "Uh,

Michelle!" he called up the stairs. "Your friends are here. And so is your pizza!"

Michelle ran down the stairs. She was wearing a long black sweatshirt and black leggings. "Thanks, Dad!"

Danny paid the delivery boy while Michelle grabbed the pizza box.

Cassie and Lee glanced around nervously as they stepped inside.

"So, Michelle," Danny said. "What's up with all the black clothes?"

Michelle thought quickly. "We're, uh, working on a play!"

"Yeah," Lee added. "For Halloween!"

"Well, have fun," Danny said. "Call me if you need me."

Danny left the room. Michelle set the pizza box on the coffee table. She and her friends sat down and took a couple of bites of pizza.

Her friends looked at her eagerly.

Michelle squirmed. It was one thing to talk about ghosts with your friends in the school cafeteria. But now she was coming down with a bad case of the jitters.

"What are we waiting for?" Cassie asked.

"Bring on the spooks!" Lee hollered, pumping his fist.

Come on, Michelle! she told herself. *Be brave!* She couldn't let her friends think she was chicken. Besides, this was going to be a lot easier with her friends along. And her dad was home if she needed to shout for help.

Michelle took a deep breath. It was now or never. She *had* to get to the bottom of this ghost business!

"Okay," she said at last. "Let's go." But then she stopped. "Wait!" She snapped her fingers and ran to the hall closet. She pulled out her dad's Dustbuster.

"What's that for?" Cassie asked.

"For catching ghosts," Michelle said. "I sure don't want to touch them. And I don't know if we can grab them anyway. Maybe we can just vacuum them up!"

"Great idea!" said Lee. "Wish I'd thought of that."

"Could I take a turn too?" Cassie asked.

Michelle grinned. Her dad thought she was just having friends over for pizza.

But that was just an excuse. "Come on, guys!" she said bravely. She revved the Dustbuster. *Vroom! Vroom!* "We've got some serious ghost-busting to do!"

Chapter 6

 "Here!" said Michelle. She pointed at the kitchen counter. "This is where the snacks were when they disappeared."

Cassie studied the counter through her magnifying glass. "Not a crumb!" she reported.

"And here," said Michelle. She unlocked and opened the kitchen window. "I'm sure something was clawing at this window during dinner last night."

"Hmm . . ." said Lee. He stuck his head out the window. He looked up. He looked around. Then he looked down at the ground. "No footprints anywhere," he said.

Michelle knelt down and opened the cabinets, one by one. She shone a flashlight all the way in the back. She kept her finger near the Dustbuster ON button. Just in case she had to vacuum something up quick!

"BOO!" someone shouted, and tickled her.

Michelle jumped and bumped her head. "Ouch!"

"Sorry, Michelle!" It was Joey. He helped her stand up. He rubbed her head. "Are you okay?"

"Sure, Joey," Michelle muttered. "I should have known ghosts don't tickle."

Joey opened the refrigerator and poked around inside. "What did you say, honey?"

"Nothing."

"What are you guys doing, anyway?" Joey asked.

Michelle glanced at her friends. "Um, we're . . ."

"Having a scavenger hunt!" Lee said quickly.

"Great!" said Joey. "Let me know if you find the mustard!" He closed the refrigerator door. His arms were filled with sandwich fixings. "I'm working on some new jokes tonight. Now I ask you. How can I be funny without my mustard?" He winked at Michelle and her friends. Then he went downstairs to his basement apartment.

Michelle and her friends examined every inch of the house downstairs. They checked behind plants and under couches and chairs. They searched through drawers and closets. They even peeked inside the dishwasher, the washing machine, and the dryer.

"What are we looking for, anyway?" Lee asked.

Michelle scratched her head. "I'm not

sure, exactly. But I'm sure we'll know it when we find it!"

They didn't find a thing.

"Maybe it's not late enough," Cassie suggested.

Lee shook his head. "I don't think your house is haunted at all, Michelle. I think it's just your imagination."

"Maybe Lee's right," said Cassie.

Michelle frowned. "My imagination isn't that good! Come on. Let's look upstairs in my bedroom."

"Oh, yeah, that must be it," Lee teased. "The ghosts were up all night haunting your house. So now they're napping— under your bed!"

Laughing, they headed for the stairs.

Bam! Behind them the front door slammed open.

The three friends screamed. Lee ducked and raised his baseball bat.

"Boy, this wind is wicked," D.J. commented as she shut the door and walked into the living room. "What are you guys screaming about?"

Lee blushed and lowered his bat.

Cassie plopped down on the bottom step.

Michelle cleared her throat. "Um . . . practicing for cheerleading tryouts?"

D.J. rolled her eyes. "Can't you do it outside?"

"But it'll be dark soon," Michelle said.

"So wait till tomorrow." D.J. bounced upstairs.

Michelle and her friends stayed put till they heard D.J.'s door close. Then they crept up the stairs too.

"We need to check behind every door," Michelle instructed her friends.

She sent Lee to investigate the linen closet.

She told Cassie to check out the bathroom.

"Michelle!" she heard Cassie cry out.

"Come here! I want to look behind the shower curtain. But I'm too scared!"

But Michelle had tiptoed into her father's room. She peered under her dad's bed. Nothing. There wasn't a single dust bunny! Her dad was that neat!

But then she saw something.

Another pair of eyes! They were looking at her from the other side of the bed!

Michelle jumped up. *"Eeeeeeek!"*

Cassie and Lee raced in. "What's wrong!"

Aunt Becky popped up from the other side of the bed. "Michelle!" she said. She brushed her long brown hair back from her face. "You scared me half to death!"

"Ditto!" said Michelle.

Aunt Becky laughed. "What are you kids doing, anyway?"

"We're playing hide-and-seek!" Michelle blurted. "What are you doing?"

"I'm looking for those rascals, Alex and Nicky!" she said. "It's their bath time. But

I think *they're* playing hide-and-seek too! Michelle, honey, if you see them—grab 'em!"

"Sure, Aunt Becky," Michelle promised.

Michelle walked out into the hall with Lee and Cassie.

"Face it, Michelle," Lee said. "Your house isn't haunted. You're just chicken! You're scared of everything these days. Maybe you have the Halloween heebie-jeebies!"

"Lee!" Cassie said. "That's not nice! Even if it's true."

"I'm not chicken!" cried Michelle. She knew in her heart that she sort of was. But she couldn't stand having her friends think that about her. That gave her extra courage. "Look. I'm going to catch a ghost tonight if it's the last thing I do!"

"If you do," cracked Lee, "it just might be the last thing you do!"

Michelle ignored him. She led her friends into her room. "Come on," she said. "Let's look in here." She started opening all her drawers.

Lee plopped down on her bed. "I don't want to hunt for ghosts anymore."

Cassie sat down beside him. "Me either. No offense, Michelle."

"But guys—"

"Want to play Monopoly?" asked Cassie.

"Yeah!" said Lee. "Come on, Michelle. Forget about this silly ghost stuff and—and . . ."

Lee's eyes almost popped out of his head.

The bed he sat on was shaking! "Hey—!"

Something grabbed Cassie's ankle—just like in the movie!

"Helllllp!!!"

Cassie and Lee ran screaming from the room. Michelle was right behind them.

"Now do you believe me?" she hollered after them.

"We believe you! We believe you!" Lee cried.

Downstairs they almost crashed into each other. Cassie grabbed her fishing net and magnifying glass. Lee picked up his goalie mask and baseball bat from the floor.

"We're done!" cried Lee. "We want to go home. Now!" He yanked open the front door.

"But wait!" Michelle cried. "Your parents aren't here yet!"

"That's okay," said Cassie as she hurried out the door. "We'll wait—on the front porch!"

Michelle followed them out to the porch. "Hey, Cassie," she said, "do you think I could spend the night at your house?"

Cassie looked at her as if she had some gross disease. As if she might bring the ghosts with her in her overnight bag! "Uh,

I don't think so!" she said nervously. "I think we're going out of town!"

Great, Michelle thought as she stood in her haunted doorway. *My friends believe me. They believe my house is haunted!* She sat down next to them to wait for their parents. The sun was setting and it was getting dark.

Michelle shivered. Soon her friends would be gone—safe and sound in their own normal houses. In their own normal beds.

But Michelle would be stuck here—in her haunted house—all night long!

Chapter

7

♥ "Stop talking about it!" Stephanie said. "You're making me scared too!"

Stephanie stuck her head under her bed. Nothing but shoes, a couple of books, and an old candy wrapper.

She checked under Michelle's bed—for the third time. Nothing but comic books and dust!

"Look," she told Michelle, "there's nothing under your bed. There's nothing under my bed. There's nothing in the closet, either!"

"But Stephanie—!"

"Michelle! You're just getting us spooked up over nothing. Okay?" Stephanie shook her head. "Maybe you should leave town till Halloween is over. Now go—to—sleep!"

Michelle watched Stephanie put on her Walkman headphones, get into bed, and pull the covers over her head.

"Mo moo meep!" Stephanie mumbled under the covers.

Michelle punched her pillow. Her friends believed her house was haunted. Why wouldn't her family believe her?

I'm not even going to try to sleep tonight, she thought. *I'm just going to lie here and wait for the ghosts to get me. But I hope they get Stephanie first!*

She started counting the roses on her wallpaper. Soon her eyelids began to droop. . . .

When she woke up, she could tell it was late.

The house was silent. Except for . . .

Yes! There was definitely somebody downstairs.

But she knew everybody was at home. And everyone should be in bed by now!

She was scared. But she was also mad. And tired! Really tired! *I know my house is haunted,* she thought. *And tonight I'm going to prove it! No matter what!*

She tiptoed to the door. "Be brave," she told herself.

She sneaked out into the hall.

Ticktock, ticktock.

Michelle peeked up at the grandfather clock. It was three minutes till midnight!

Then she listened.

Something was definitely moving around downstairs.

Whatever it was . . . it was in the kitchen.

Michelle crept down the stairs. She was careful to skip the third step from the bottom. The one that creaked.

She reached the last step—and stopped. Whistling!

Michelle frowned. Whistling? Whoever heard of a whistling ghost?

Then she laughed. Of course. It was her father! She went to find him. She could use an extra hug. And it was quiet now. Maybe she could talk to him about all the frightening things that had been going on.

She opened the kitchen door.

And stopped dead in her tracks.

Her father was in the kitchen. At least, it looked like her father. His face looked strange in the soft glow from the tiny light over the stove. Uncle Jesse's goofy black spider dangled above his head. He was stirring something. A big cast-iron kettle full of something steaming and bubbling . . .

He frowned into the pages of a book. Michelle could read the title:

KITCHEN MAGIC
Supernatural Spells
and
Bewitching Brews

Bong! Bong! Bong!

The grandfather clock continued to chime the hour.

Bong! Bong! Bong!

Midnight. The witching hour!

Michelle gasped.

Danny's eyes flicked up from the book. His face looked eerie in the shadows. "Michelle," he called. He wiggled his eyebrows up and down. "Come, taste my new brew. . . ."

"No!" cried Michelle. Her legs seemed to turn into overcooked spaghetti. She wanted to run—but she couldn't move!

It's happening, she thought. *Just like in the movie. My father has been taken over by evil spirits!*

Michelle sank to the floor and began to sob.

"Michelle!" said Danny. He hurried over and pulled her to her feet. "Honey—what's wrong?"

Michelle couldn't speak. She was crying too hard. She pointed at the bubbling brew on the stove.

Danny frowned, puzzled. "You're crying about my new recipe for vegetable soup? I thought you liked vegetable soup."

"B-but that book!" Michelle cried.

Danny glanced at the cover and laughed. "I'm not cooking from *this!* I'm just reading it. And it's hilarious!"

Danny drew Michelle to the table and made her sit down.

"Uh, just a minute, honey." He grabbed a damp dishcloth from the sink. He wiped the table, then dried it with a dish towel. "There, that's better." He put a bookmark in his book and laid it down.

"This book is by a guest who's appearing on my show."

"Your show?" said Michelle. Her dad was on the TV show *Good Morning, San Francisco*. He worked with Aunt Becky. Part of their job was to interview interesting people.

Danny nodded. "It's sort of a Halloween gag. I'm just reading it to get ready for my interview. So I'll know what kind of questions to ask. Boy, what a kooky guy," he added. "Can you believe anybody really *believes* this stuff?"

Michelle started to laugh—and cry, at the same time. She couldn't hold in her scary, mixed-up feelings anymore.

She told her father everything. About how scary the movie *Haunted Houseful* was. About how scared she'd been all week. How she couldn't sleep. How she couldn't stay awake at school. And how she and her friends had tried to track down the ghosts tonight.

"Oh, Michelle!" said Danny. He hugged her tight. "You must have felt terrible! You should have told me!"

"I tried to," said Michelle. "But no one believed me. I tried to tell Stephanie. She told me to go to sleep. I even told you. But you thought I was joking."

Danny spread a dish towel over his shoulder. Then he let Michelle sob until her tears ran dry.

Aunt Becky came in, yawning. "Hey, is Michelle okay?"

"Yeah," said Danny. "She's gonna be. Maybe some hot cocoa would help."

"I'll make it," said Aunt Becky. She got out the milk, sugar, and cocoa. "Ready in a minute."

Michelle wiped her eyes on the edge of the dish towel. "Thanks, Dad."

"Anytime," said Danny. "Now. Time for Dad Talk number forty-three."

Michelle just sighed. She knew what was coming.

"I hate to say I told you so, honey," Danny said gently. "But wasn't I right about going to see that movie? Wasn't it too scary?"

Michelle nodded. "Yeah, you were right. The PG doesn't stand for Pretty Goofy. It stands for Pretty Gross!"

Danny and Aunt Becky laughed.

"I guess I'm just not ready for scary movies yet," Michelle added.

"Maybe you'll never be," said Aunt Becky. "I'm grown up, and I still don't like scary movies. They give me the creeps. They give me bad dreams, too."

"Really?" asked Michelle.

"Really!" said Aunt Becky.

"Doesn't Uncle Jesse tease you about being chicken?"

"Sure!" said Becky. "But I just make a joke out of it. I'm not going to let him push me into going. Not when I know it's something I don't want to see." She handed Michelle a cup of steaming hot chocolate. "Besides, he can always get Joey to go. Joey likes scary movies. He thinks they're funny."

Michelle gave her a hug. "Thanks, Aunt Becky."

"Feel better now, pumpkin?" Danny asked.

Michelle smiled. "Uh-huh." She took a sip of the hot chocolate. "But I still say our house is haunted."

"Michelle!" Danny shook his head. "Honey, there's no such thing as ghosts. They're just . . . just stories based on fear and superstition."

"But Dad! I'm telling you it's true! That's why Cassie and Lee were so frightened when they came over for pizza tonight. They saw the ghosts too!"

Danny looked her in the eye. "Saw the ghosts?"

"Well, not exactly," Michelle admitted. "But Lee and Cassie were sitting on my bed. And the bed started shaking. Just like in the movie! And then something grabbed Cassie around the ankle!"

"Uh, Michelle," Aunt Becky said. "Was that around six o'clock tonight?"

Michelle nodded.

Aunt Becky grinned. "I think I found your ghosts," she said. "In fact, I put them in the tub right after that! Honey, that's where I found Nicky and Alex. Remember? They were hiding because they didn't want to take a bath."

"Oh." Michelle sighed. "Wait! The other day my snack disappeared from the counter in the kitchen. That kind of stuff happened in the movie, too."

"I think I can explain that," said Danny. "Was Comet around when your snack disappeared?"

Michelle thought back. "I guess so," she had to admit. "But Comet has been acting really weird too. I think he knows the house is haunted."

Danny nodded. "I took Comet to the

vet today. Remember? He wasn't eating his dog food. And he threw up once. The vet said there was nothing wrong with him except an upset stomach and . . . er, other digestive problems. He's been eating too many snacks and junk food. He probably stole your snacks when you weren't looking."

Michelle sighed. "But he's been acting so weird. . . ."

"He just wasn't feeling well," said Danny. "That's all."

"Maybe that's not the only reason," Michelle insisted. "I've been hearing weird sounds every night. Maybe that's why he's acting strange. Maybe—"

"No, Michelle," Danny said firmly. "I think you're letting that movie and all the Halloween hoopla get to you. You're just letting your fears color how you see the world. Things seem more frightening when we have a fearful attitude. But scary things can always be explained.

"I promise you, Michelle," Danny went on. "Our house is not—"

"YIIIKES! HELLLLP! DAD!" Stephanie screamed as she ran into the kitchen. "Come quick!"

Danny jumped to his feet. "Stephanie! What is it? What's the matter?"

Stephanie gasped for breath. She stared at her father with terrified eyes. "There's a ghost in Michelle's closet!"

Chapter 8

 "Michelle!" Stephanie shrieked. "You were right! There is something in our room."

Michelle smiled smugly. "See? I told you guys!" *Finally someone believes me,* Michelle thought. But then—a thought popped into her head. "D-does that mean our house *is* haunted?"

"What's going on?" Joey asked as he burst into the kitchen.

Jesse wandered in with one eye barely open. "Is everybody okay?" he mumbled sleepily.

Aunt Becky grinned. She grabbed him before he wandered out the back door. "Everything's fine," she told him. "Except Michelle says our house is haunted."

"Haunted?" mumbled Jesse.

"Haunted!" exclaimed Joey. "Okay. What's the joke?"

"No joke!" Michelle insisted. "It's true."

"D-d-dad! Please believe me!" Stephanie begged. "There's something in our closet. Come look!"

"What makes you so sure there's a ghost up there?"

"Because—I—" Stephanie took a few deep breaths. "I heard it. It sounded like a dead person . . . scratching on the walls . . . moaning *ow, ow!*"

"Do something, Dad!" Michelle begged.

Danny was starting to look nervous. Joey and Jesse put their arms across his shoulders.

"Okay, men!" Joey commanded. "We've

got a closet to unspook! Let's go get that ghost!"

Danny put on a brave face. He pulled the belt to his bathrobe tight. He turned off the stove. Then he grabbed a wire whisk and charged up the stairs.

Everyone else in the Tanner household followed.

The twins were clapping at the top of the stairs. They had climbed out of their beds. Now they were shouting as if it were a great big game.

Down the hall Comet was barking wildly. He was still locked up in Danny's bathroom. Stephanie ran ahead and let him out. "We might need him for protection," she said.

D.J. stumbled out into the hall. "What's happening? Is it another earthquake?"

"Nope," said Michelle. "It's a ghost. In my closet!"

"There's no room in your closet for a

ghost," D.J. mumbled sleepily. "It's too messy."

The whole family stumbled into Michelle and Stephanie's bedroom. They stopped in front of Michelle's closet door.

For a moment no one said or did anything. They just stared at the door.

A soft, high-pitched "Owwww!" split the silence. It was definitely coming from the closet!

The girls screamed.

Jesse shrieked and grabbed Aunt Becky.

Danny reached for the knob.

"Wait!" Michelle cried. She grabbed her father's hand. She wanted desperately to show the others that there really was a ghost. But now she was terrified. It was all too real. What would happen if they let it out?

"Maybe we shouldn't open the door," she whispered.

"Why not?" D.J. whispered back.

"It might get us," Michelle said. "It

might be mad that we want to get rid of it! It might—"

"Michelle," said her father. "We've got to get to the bottom of this. Now step aside."

Joey held Comet, who was barking and jumping wildly. "Don't worry, Michelle. Comet will protect us!"

"Come here, honey," Aunt Becky said. "Stand next to me."

Michelle stood back and clutched Aunt Becky's bathrobe.

Jesse held Nicky and Alex.

Stephanie grabbed D.J.

Danny gripped his wire whisk over his head. With his other hand he reached for the doorknob. His fingers trembled.

Michelle closed her eyes so she wouldn't see anything. Then she opened one eye so she wouldn't miss anything.

Danny turned the doorknob . . . and slowly . . . slowly . . . opened the closet door. . . .

Chapter 9

 "Me-ow!"

Comet strained to pounce inside.

"Me-owwww!"

For a moment no one said a word. They just stared into the messy, dark closet.

"Kittens!" cried Aunt Becky. "I hear kittens."

"Ghost kittens?" asked Michelle.

"No, honey," said Becky. "It sounds like regular kittens."

She and Michelle crept into the closet. The Tanner house was an old house. The closet had a small door at the back. The top of it came up to Michelle's waist. No one knew exactly what it was for. Maybe it was a place to hide valuables. Or maybe it was just extra storage.

Slowly Aunt Becky opened the door.

"Meow! Me-ow!"

"Oh, Aunt Becky!" Michelle whispered. "Look!"

There they were. Curled up way in the back. In a nest of wadded-up old clothes.

A beautiful black cat—with a white half-moon shape on her forehead. Nursing at her side were five newborn kittens. They were colored different combinations of white and black.

Michelle's eyes glowed. "Can I hold one, Aunt Becky?"

Becky shook her head and put her finger to her lips. "Not just yet," she whispered. "Mama cats are pretty protective of their new babies. Let's just let them be for now."

She and Michelle quietly backed out of the closet.

Danny was shaking his head in amazement. "I can't believe there are kittens in there!"

"That must be Miss Teasdale's cat," Michelle said.

"But how did she get in there?" Stephanie asked.

Danny shrugged. "This is an old house. She could have sneaked into the basement somehow. Then she could have slipped around at night looking for the right spot."

D.J. grinned. "That's where the scratching sounds were coming from!"

"Maybe Midnight was hungry," said Michelle. "Maybe she was looking for the snacks we keep stashed in there."

Stephanie groaned. "Michelle!"

"Oh, really?" Danny said. "We'll talk about that later!" He quietly shut the door. "Can Comet sleep in the basement with you tonight, Joey?"

"I'd be delighted," said Joey. "Come on, Comet. I've got this great video about a Saint Bernard. I've been dying to show you . . ."

Danny put his arm around Michelle's shoulders.

"Hey, Dad," she said. "Can we go call Miss Teasdale?"

"Well, I don't know, honey," Danny said. "It's after midnight."

"I know," said Michelle. "But what if Comet were missing? And someone found him. Wouldn't you want to know right away?"

Danny grinned. "You're right. Let's go give her a call."

Miss Teasdale was still up when they phoned her. She was watching *Dracula* on the late-late show.

She was delighted to know her cat was safe and sound. And she couldn't wait to see the kittens. Danny invited her to come over in the morning as soon as she was up. "In fact, why don't you join us for breakfast?"

Then he handed the phone to Michelle.

"Michelle, my dear," Miss Teasdale said. "Midnight must have sensed she would be safe in your closet. Would you like to have one of her kittens? When they're old enough, of course."

"Really?" Michelle cried. Then her smile faded. "Oh, Miss Teasdale. I'd love to. But I guess I can't. Comet would just want to chase it all the time. But can I come visit them?"

"Of course you may! You are most welcome, anytime." She paused a moment, then added, "How would you like to name one?"

Michelle squealed—but from happiness this time. "I'd love to! Thanks, Miss Teasdale. See you in the morning!"

That night Michelle fell asleep the minute her head hit the pillow. Nothing could keep her awake. Not even a little scratching and meowing!

The next morning Miss Teasdale came over. She brought Danny a basket of jams and scones and English tea to add to the breakfast.

But first Michelle took Miss Teasdale up to her room.

Quietly they peeked into the closet.

"Oh, my!" Miss Teasdale whispered when she saw the kittens. "Aren't they beautiful? And a perfect present for Halloween."

Michelle nodded.

"Well, Michelle. I have several names I'm thinking of. But would you like to go first? Have you thought of any names?"

"I sure have," Michelle whispered. "See the white one in the middle there? The one with one black paw?"

Miss Teasdale laughed softly. "She looks as if she stepped in a puddle of ink."

Michelle giggled. "I thought of a name for her right before I went to sleep."

"Yes?"

"Spooky!" Michelle announced.

"Perfect!" Miss Teasdale agreed.

✦✦✦✦✦✦✦✦✦✦✦✦

For information about
Mary-Kate + Ashley's Fun Club™,
the Olsen Twins' only
official fan club, write to:

Mary-Kate + Ashley's Fun Club™
859 Hollywood Way, Suite 412
Burbank, California 91505

✦✦✦✦✦✦✦✦✦✦✦✦

FULL HOUSE™
Michelle

#1: THE GREAT PET PROJECT

#2: THE SUPER-DUPER SLEEPOVER PARTY

#3: MY TWO BEST FRIENDS

#4: LUCKY, LUCKY DAY

#5: THE GHOST IN MY CLOSET

Based on the Hit TV Series!

Available from

A MINSTREL® BOOK

Published by Pocket Books

Join eight-year old Nancy
and her best friends as they
collect clues and solve mysteries in

THE
NANCY DREW
NOTEBOOKS™

#1: THE SLUMBER PARTY SECRET
#2: THE LOST LOCKET
#3: THE SECRET SANTA
#4: BAD DAY FOR BALLET
#5: THE SOCCER SHOE CLUE
#6: THE ICE CREAM SCOOP
#7: TROUBLE AT CAMP TREEHOUSE
#8: THE BEST DETECTIVE
#9: THE THANKSGIVING SURPRISE

by Carolyn Keene
Illustrated by Anthony Accardo

A MINSTREL® BOOK

Published by Pocket Books

1045-03